Making a Difference–Making Saving a Habit!

Dear Parent, Grandparent, Educator, and Concerned Adult:

Providing children, parents, educators, and community leaders, strategic, wholesome, fun, educational, and relevant financial literacy tools is one of the primary purposes of the It's A Habit! Company, Inc. (IAHC). At IAHC, we have a clear mission: **Changing Children's Lives One Dime at a Time!**

IAHC believes that in order to accomplish our mission and effectively address a growing national financial literacy problem, it is essential to start exposing children to solid financial habits at an early age prior to their forming life-long debilitating attitudes and habits toward money. IAHC believes this is critical because: (1) as humans, we are creatures of habit; and (2) studies reflect that advertisers are increasingly targeting children at earlier and earlier ages, making it more difficult for us to influence them as they grow older.

IAHC further believes that the most important and empowering financial message anyone can be taught is to pay themselves first. Both the **saving is a habit** and **from every dollar save a dime** messages that IAHC teaches are child- and adult-friendly translations of the **pay yourself first** philosophy. IAHC believes that people who pay themselves first rarely, if ever, find themselves in financial difficulty. Additionally, IAHC believes that people who pay themselves first go on to own homes and businesses and are better prepared to help others. Ultimately, people who learn to save are better positioned to participate in the American dream regardless of their social, ethnic, or economic background.

We hope you and your children enjoy Sammy's adventures and that they provide the catalyst for many thoughtful conversations. And of course, we hope the entire family makes saving a habit!

Sam X Renick

Sam X Renick
CEO & Founder
The It's A Habit! Company, Inc.

Thank You!

The **It's A Habit! Company, Inc**. is run by a group of dedicated men, women, and children, who believe in and are dedicated to fulfilling the company mission. The Company is also supported by numerous volunteers. Without their commitment neither Sammy nor his adventures would be possible.

Art Direction and Editing
Alto Studio – Carlos Rodriguez
Special thanks to the entire Rodriguez family: Leticia, Ynez, and Yzacc

Story Consultant and Guidance
Victor Gonzalez

Story Contributors
Yvette Raymond, Monique Renick, Greg Renick, Alonso Silva Jr.

Support
Gerardo Acosta, Carol Alvarado, Chi Chan, Eddie Chan, Christopher Ferebee,
The Gonzalez Family, Olga Acosta Lentine, Loyola Marymount University,
Ernesto Pantoja, Stephen Pina, Janos Pomazzi, The Renick Family, Rose Roeder,
Mike Sala, Lynn Scarborough, The Silva Family, The Stevens Family,
Father Carmine Vairo, Councilmen Benjamin "Frank" Venti, Oscar de Villegas

Dedication
To all the great people who make up, believe in, and execute the It's A Habit! vision.

Remembrance
In honor of the crew of
Columbia
February 1, 2003

The Adventures of Sammy the Saver
in
Will Sammy Ride the World's First Space Coaster?

Written by Sam X Renick · Illustrated by Juan Alvarado

Changing Children's Lives One Dime at a Time

"It's A Habit!"
Company, Inc.

Los Angeles, California

Predict the Chapter Titles

A strategic, fun, and unique feature of this book is that readers get to predict chapter titles. Successful readers use strategies like predicting. Predicting helps readers to think seriously about what they are reading and to improve their comprehension.

The total number of words in each chapter title is located in parentheses below. Clues are contained in each chapter to guide you toward the choice the author has made for each chapter title. If you can find the main idea of each chapter, you will probably correctly predict the chapter title. Just in case you need them, the answers can be found on the last page of each chapter. Good luck!

Contents

It all began the day after holiday vacation ended.

"Boys and girls, I have fantastic news!" said our teacher, Mrs. Gold. "We won the space science essay contest."

"All right!" we cheered.

"The prize is that we all get a chance to ride the world's first space coaster," she said.

I began to daydream about the fantastic news.

"Calm down, kids. There are two conditions," said Mrs. Gold. "You will need permission to go from your parents; and you will also need three-hundred dollars each."

The news was so fantastic that I did not stop dreaming to think about where I would get three-hundred dollars.

Were you able to predict the title of **Chapter One?**

Fantastic News

As soon as the bell rang, I ran home as fast as I could.

"Mama! Papa!" I yelled.

"They're not home," said my brother Garbanzo.

"Guess who is going to ride the world's first space coaster?" I bragged.

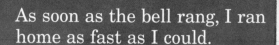

"Huh?" said Garbanzo.

"I just need permission to go and three-hundred dollars," I said.

"Not a chance," laughed Garbanzo. "Mama and Papa will never give you permission and three-hundred dollars."

Just then, my parents came home.

"Mama! Papa!" I began. "My class won the space science essay contest. We get to ride the world's first space coaster. May I go? The whole trip only costs three-hundred dollars. May I go?"

"Three-hundred dollars!" gasped Papa.

"Pleeeeease, Papa?" I begged. "I will never ask for anything again."

"You cannot give him three-hundred dollars," said Garbanzo.

That was when I jumped on Garbanzo and tackled him.

"Sammy, get off your brother!" said Mama.
"Let Papa and me talk this over."

Were you able to predict the title of **Chapter Two?**
Permission and Three Hundred Dollars

Chapter Three

____Is a____!

That night Papa said, "Sammy, I know that winning the essay contest was not easy."

"No, Papa, it was hard," I said.

"Mama and I have decided to give you half the money for the trip from our savings account, if you save the other half. Can you do it?"

I remembered the secret
Auntie Squirly had taught me:
Saving is a habit!

"I can do it!" I said.

The announcement startled Garbanzo.
"You must be kidding, right Sammy?
You will never be able to save
one-hundred-fifty dollars in time for
the trip."

"I only need to save one-hundred
dollars," I said. "I already have
fifty dollars in my savings account."

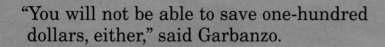

"You will not be able to save one-hundred dollars, either," said Garbanzo.

"Maybe Sammy can save the money," said my sisters Dyme and Penny.

"No, he can't."

"Yes, he can!"

"Cannot!"

"Can, too!"

I left them arguing and ran down the hall to my room. I had to make a plan. I counted the days on my calendar. It was exactly one-hundred days to blast off. *If I save one dollar a day, I can go,* I thought.

"Saving is a habit!" I said to my dog Nickel. **"Saving is a habit**. I can do this."

"Woof!" replied Nickel. (I took that as a yes.)

Were you able to predict the title of **Chapter Three?**

Chapter Four
Do Not _____ _____!

I worked and saved every day for weeks.
I did not stop even to play with my friends.

Everything was all right until some of the kids in my class lined up early one morning to buy their tickets for the space coaster.

"Sammy," they asked. "When are you going to buy your ticket?"

"I am not sure," I said. "I have to save some more money first. How did you save your money so fast?"

"We did not need to," they replied. "Our parents just gave us the money."

Snap! I broke the pencil
I was holding.

"That is not fair," I growled.

"Take it easy, Sammy," said
my friend, Jammer. "Breaking
your pencil will not help.
But we could work and save
together. That might help."

"We could try, I guess," I sighed.

Read
and
Succeed

16

When I got home, Mama knew
something was wrong.

"Sammy, you look sad. What is
wrong?"

"Other kids are already buying
their tickets for the space trip,"
I said. "I will never be able to save
enough money in time to go."

17

"Things are not always easy, Sammy," said Mama. "But you can do anything you want to if you work hard, and do not give up."

"Your mama is right, Sammy," said Auntie Squirly. "Do not give up! Keep working toward your goal. You will make it."

"All right," I grinned. "I'll keep trying."

18

That night, I dreamed about the space
coaster. I was racing through space, past
moons, meteors, and stars."

But suddenly the dream turned into a nightmare.

"You won't be able to save one-hundred dollars," teased Garbanzo.

That is it! I thought. I will save more than one-hundred dollars, no matter what.

Were you able to predict the title of **Chapter Four?**
Do Not Give Up!

Chapter Five
_ Did _!

In order to save more, I decided not to buy some of my favorite things like ice cream, candy, and baseball caps. *Keep saving!* I told myself. I was more determined than ever to ride the world's first space coaster.

Finally, the last day to buy a ticket had arrived.

"I do not think I have saved enough money,"
I said to Nickel. I held my breath as the teller
counted my money.

"Ten, twenty, thirty, fifty, one-hundred,
one-hundred-fifty, two-hundred dollars."

"I did it!" I shouted. "Nickel, I did it!"

I raced home with Nickel barking and chasing me.

"Mama! Papa!" I yelled. "I did it! I did it! I saved an extra one-hundred-fifty dollars! I have two-hundred dollars in all! With the one-hundred-fifty you gave me, I have fifty dollars more than I need. I can go!"

Thump!

Everyone looked around. Garbanzo had fainted.

Were you able to predict the title of **Chapter Five?**
I Did It!

Just then, the phone rang.

"Sammy, I have bad news," said Jammer. "I cannot go. I still need twenty-five dollars more."

"Hold on, Jammer," I said. "Mama, may I give Jammer twenty-five dollars so he can ride the space coaster, too?"

"Sammy, it's your money. You saved it," said Mama. "You may give it to Jammer if you want to."

"Jammer, you can go!" I said. "I have twenty-five dollars I can give you."

"No way!" said Jammer. "Really?"

"Yes, really," I said. "It would not be fun riding the space coaster without you."

Jammer spent the night at my house.

"Can you believe it?" I asked. "Tomorrow we will be riding in the world's first space coaster!"

"I can hardly wait!" said Jammer.

"Me, either," I said.

Just like in my dream,
we went flying past stars,
meteors, and the moons
of planets far from Earth.

"Yahoo!" I yelled.

"Ahhhhhhhh.
I think I am getting
sick," said Jammer.

"Hold on," I said to
my friend. "The ride
is almost over.
I cannot wait to tell
Garbanzo about it.
He will probably
faint again."

As we rode home, I pointed out the window. "Jammer, I want to go there next."

Jammer grinned and said, "You will get there sooner than you think, Sammy, if you just keep remembering what Auntie Squirly says."

"Right!" I laughed. **"Saving is a habit!"**

Were you able to predict the title of **Chapter Six?**
Riding the Space Coaster